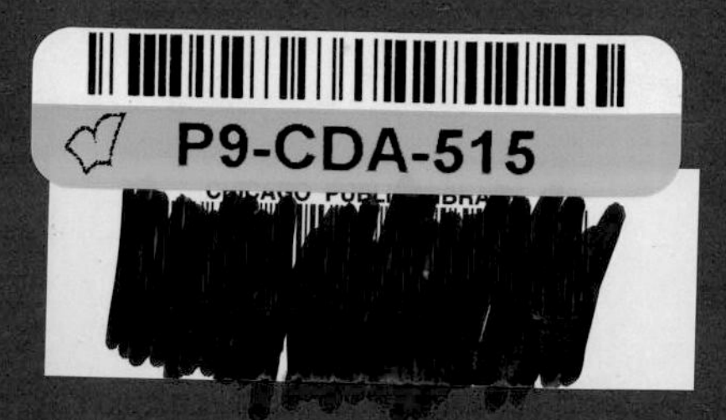
P9-CDA-515

MOUSE'S FIRST HALLOWEEN

Lauren Thompson

ILLUSTRATED BY

Buket Erdogan

SIMON & SCHUSTER

BOOKS FOR YOUNG READERS

NEW YORK • LONDON

TORONTO • SYDNEY • SINGAPORE

To
Owen
L.T.

To my
daughter,
Yagmur
B.E.

SIMON & SCHUSTER BOOKS FOR YOUNG READERS

One spooky night
when the moon was bright,
Mouse crept around,
and this is what he found....

High in the sky,
Mouse saw
something flying—
Flit! Flit! Flit!

"Eeek!"
Mouse
squeaked.

What could it be?

Swooping bats!

That's all.

Not so scary after all.

Down on the ground,
Mouse heard something moving—
Rustle! Rustle! Rustle!

"Eeek!" Mouse squeaked.

What could it be?

Tumbling leaves!
That's all.
Not so scary after all.

Up on a pole,
Mouse saw
something flapping—
Flip! Flip! Flip!

"Eeek!"
Mouse squeaked.

What could it be?

A waving scarecrow!

That's all.

Not so scary after all.

Under a branch,
Mouse heard
something dropping—
Plop! Plop! Plop!

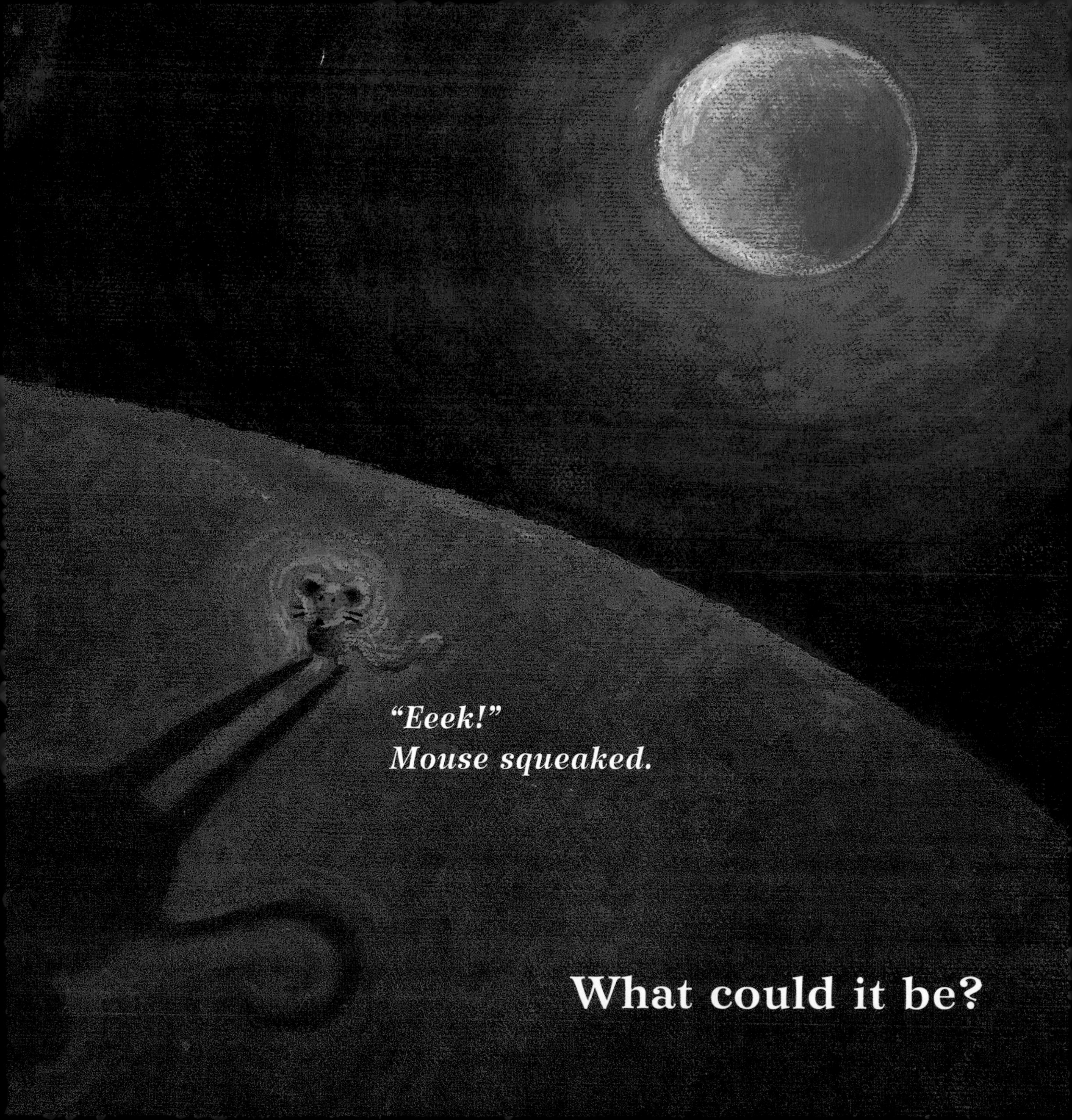

"Eeek!"
Mouse squeaked.

What could it be?

Falling apples!

That's all.

Not so scary after all.

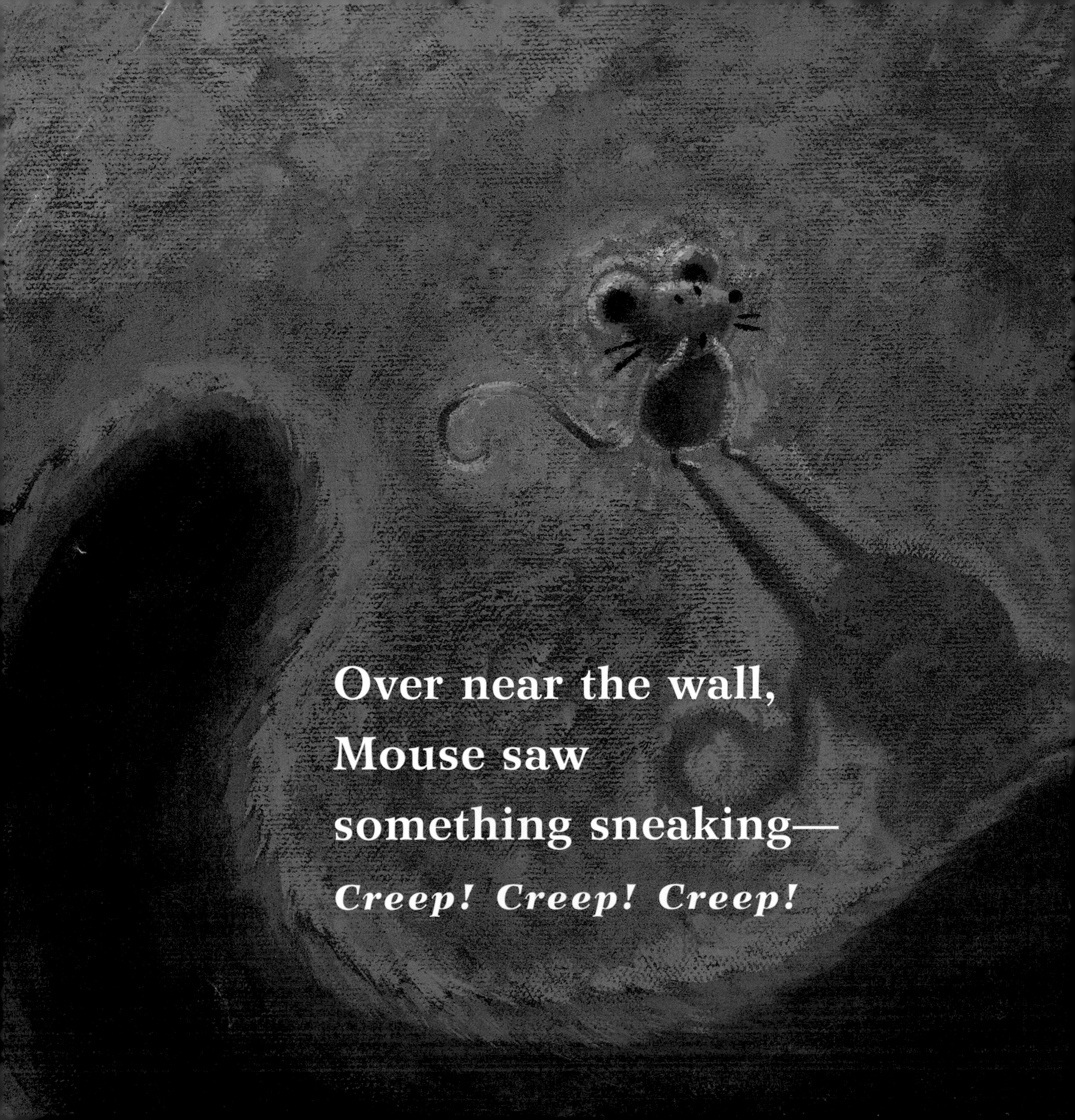

Over near the wall,
Mouse saw
something sneaking—
Creep! Creep! Creep!

“Eeek!”
Mouse
squeaked.

What could it be?

Scampering kittens!

That's all.
Not so scary
after all.

Deep in the shadows,
Mouse saw something flickering—
Grin! Grin! Grin!

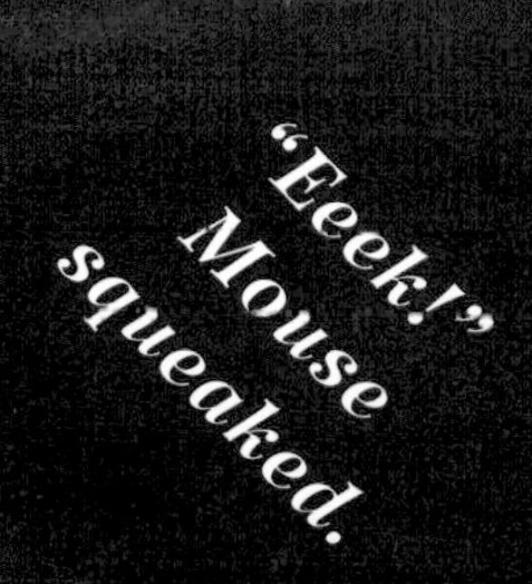

"Eeek!" Mouse squeaked.

What could it be?

A glowing

jack
- o'-
lantern!

That's all.
Not so scary
after all.

Then, on the step,
Mouse heard something knocking—
Thump! Thump! Thump!

"Eeek!"
Mouse
squeaked.

What, oh, what could it be?

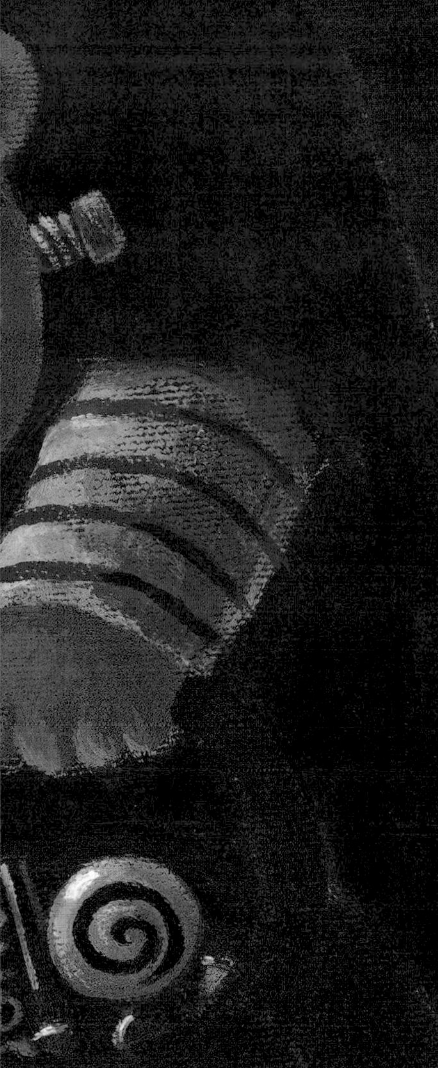

TRICK-OR-TREATERS!

Hooray!

And they sang,

"Trick or treat!

Giggle and fright!

It's fun to be scared...

on Halloween night!”